In Solitude

Thoughts and feelings of an 11 year old during the coronavirus pandemic

Apala Banerjee

This book would not be possible without the motivation and support from my parents. Thank you Ma and Baa.

The music in my heart I bore,
Long after it was heard no more.
William Wordsworth, The Reaper

Contents

Preface

Before December of 2019, no one knew of COVID-19.

No one knew how this tiny virus, somewhere in China, would turn the world upside down. No one knew that COVID-19 would claim the lives of several hundred thousand people worldwide. No one knew that COVID-19 would prevent people of the entire world from setting foot outside their homes. It was a tiny virus that disrupted the world.

I sat at home, during shelter in place, while the news caused earthquakes in my head every time the tv was on. My rushing, quick-paced life was halted without warning. It was like there was a bottomless pit in my path. I couldn't fathom anything; my mind was a blizzard of questions. During these moments of "self-reflection", I penned a few lines daily. It grew into this book.

Readers, I hope you like my book: <u>In Solitude</u>.

1. Suddenly One Day

March 25th, 2020

I was in the middle of my busy activities of sixth grade,
but COVID has made all of that fade.
I was thrown into my house with the door locked.
All my perception, thoughts, feelings were blocked.

One day, I was happily going to school,
and the next day, online learning was the rule.
One day, I had afterschool in full swing,
and the next day, I no longer play my violin or sing.

One day I was sitting with my peer,
and the next day, my friends were no longer near.
One day I went to the mall without hesitation,
and the next day I am frightened of public transportation.

COVID halted my life without permission,
and, unlike a movie's intermission,
I do not know if I will get my life back.
Will I get everything back on track?

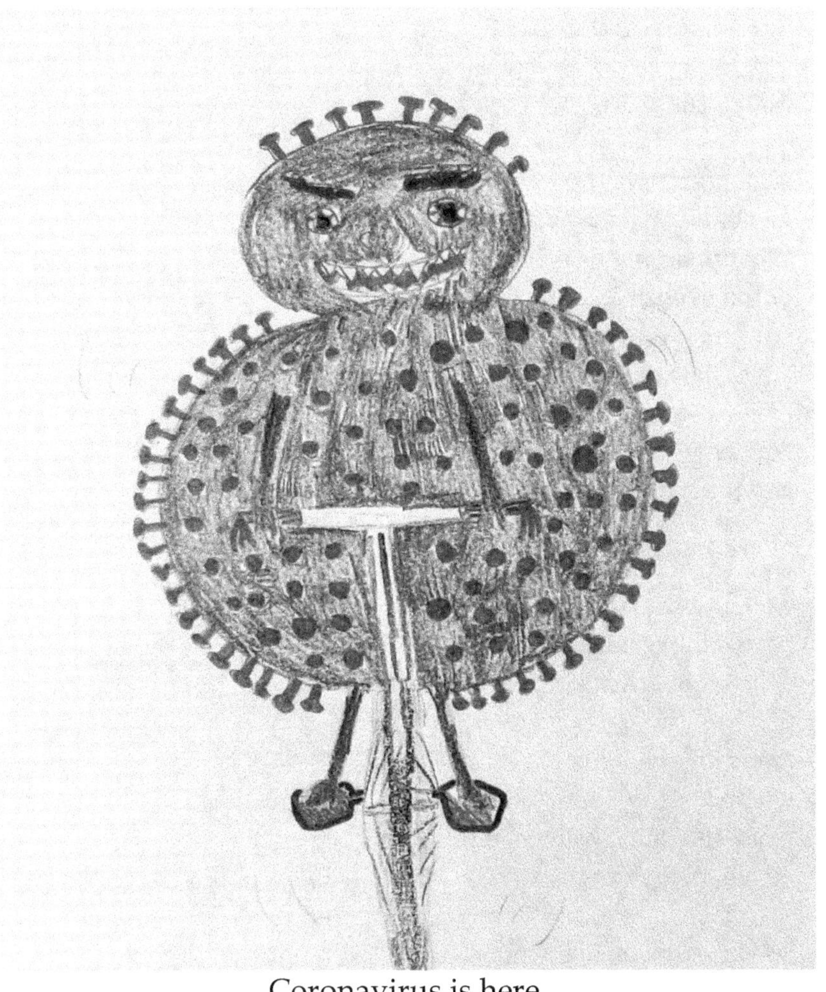

Coronavirus is here

2. I Miss You, School

March 26th, 2020

When there was no more school,
my tears could fill a pool.
What to do when you can't meet your peer,
or the quench for knowledge isn't near?

I miss the crowded halls.
I miss all the annoying boys' calls.
I miss my hard, grey locker,
and the scolding of a continuing talker.

I miss my teacher's smile,
which I would look at, all the while.
I listen to the advice and knowledge they pour,
which I could listen to, for hours more.

I miss my every friend,
whom I talk to, for days on the end.
I miss their ridiculous chatter.
To me, it does matter.

So, this is my middle school,
full of fun, love, and rule.
Instead of my peer or teacher,
I have to stare at a cold metallic computer.

Waiting outside the school at the carpool line.

3. Locked, Alone and Waiting

March 27th, 2020

COVID has locked all my doors,
with my tears, I'll flood the floors.
I cannot be stuck at home anymore!
This confinement, I cannot ignore.

I am frustrated and bored.
I can't find my computer's cord.
Online school dumps work each day.
I don't find any time to play.

My neighbors have all the fun,
with water balloons and the water gun.
I have to work each day.
Why can't the pandemic go away!?

How long will I be at home?
When can I at the park roam?
When will I see my friends?
When will this end?
When will I see the sidewalk flowers bloom?
How long will I just pace in my room?
When like the old times, will I see everyone unmasked and about?
The answer is, until the vaccine is out.

4. Virus Everywhere

March 28th, 2020

Shelter in place isn't a cake walk,
because you can't believe some people talk.
Some news is but true,
like there are three thousand hospital beds too few.

Here something very crazy;
(it won't be done by those who are lazy).
Wash all the groceries like dishes,
and to not freeze the box of fishes.

To rid coronavirus from the grocery,
one must wash everything, from carrots to celery.
The produce will soak in baking soda,
while cleaning the packaging is a Clorox extravaganza!

After two hours spent,
you wish you went,
straight to the farm or factory;
Then you wouldn't have to clean your grocery.

5. Nature is Unstoppable

March 29th, 2020

I can't go out the door,
but nature will grow more and more!

My neighbor has a vegetable patch,
which will sprout and grow.
Hey critters! it has no latch,
all its veggies you can tow!

My neighbor has a small hill,
which is lush and green.
With flowers it will fill,
and visiting birds will be seen!

Today COVID is not on my mind,
I must let myself from that bind.

6. The Tech of Tomorrow

March 30th, 2020

I must put myself at ease,
and not think about the disease.

What will happen in the future?
When robots will be the worker?
What will humans do?
Relax and watch the metal crew?

How can one made of wire,
cook, clean and start a fire?
Even if it's advanced and new,
it's still a box of steel and screw.

It can't be an iron probe,
which will run the complex globe!
Can engineers make a living man?
(Let's enjoy that while we can!)

7. The Big Apple Weeps

March 31st, 2020

Mother Nature, think twice,
before you put us on thin ice.
Even those who don't suffer COVID's pain,
will surely go insane.

But what can I say?
My restriction is no peer play.
I sympathize with those who are ill,
Why can't pharmacies just make a pill?

Even NYC doctors cry,
to save patients' lives, they try.
The virus is like a wildfire,
it'll conquer every empire.

A vaccine is our only hope,
that researcher's find under the microscope.

8. Let me Out!

April 1st, 2020

COVID has locked and shut all doors,
and being stuck at home really bores.
What to do when you've got only a roof above your head?
One could stare at that instead.

I am not used to living all day in a house,
it has risks from weeds to a mouse.
Then there was a horror in the yard,
to believe it, will be hard.

The yard has a certain pink blossom.
I thought it was awesome.
But it is an edible weed!
The gardener gave us no warning to heed!

The weed is strong; roots in the ground.
Everywhere it is found.
Everywhere it has dispersed its seed!
I will vanquish this weed.

9. The Bright Side

April 2nd, 2020

COVID 19 won't stop us.
We'll just not use the bus.
This isn't all a sour line.
It is a chance for family time.

We are stuck in COVID's mist,
But will make a Spotify playlist.
COVID will give us a fright,
but we'll watch Netflix all night.

COVID will give a scare,
but we are family, so we care.
I am glad I have my iPad,
Otherwise I would be sad.

10. Let's be Patient

April 3rd, 2020

With shelter in place in my way,
I have been trying to brighten my day.
In my hands, a spade and hose.
My observation grows.

Nature makes many a blunder,
but the sky doesn't ring with thunder.
Nature doesn't fuss, neither should we.
It will make you calm, guarantee!

On a branch, different colors of a single flower.
The bush didn't shake and cower.
Nature didn't fuss, still blue was the sea,
green was the leaves on every tree.

But people! An error and we shout!
Tantrums and we pout and pout.
Like the Sphinx has been dunked in slime!
Calm down and correct it next time!

So isn't such a sour lime,
that there is no vaccine available this time.
So calm down, take rest,
researchers are doing their best!

All the best minds of the world,
have their brows furled.
They pour their knowledge into the petri dish,
with the vaccine, COVID will no longer flourish!

It will be no wonder,
next spring, the bush will repeat the blunder.

The mismatched flowers will draw a crowd,
together and healthy, we will cheer out loud!

11. Hold Your Horses

April 4th, 2020

People aren't doing shelter in place!
They will lose the COVID race!
One went to their Botox physician!
They neglected the COVID mission!

One went for a physical test!
They put in danger all the rest!
One went to the cigar store!
They need motivation to the core!

One went for the shower of the baby!
They don't care for themselves, may be!
This is self-isolation,
not summer vacation!

12. The Words I Fear

April 5th, 2020

I've heard many sounds, like a car horn,
from the time I was born.
Like the owl who, hoots every eve,
although it is gone, once I leave.

Like a soft, graceful chime,
or the rolling of a dime.
Like the groan of a chair,
at every meal, everywhere.

Like the rustling of a tree,
when the wind runs free.
I am glad the sound I hear,
have fallen on a deserving ear.

Although of all the sounds, I have heard,
from cars to a bird,
the worst word I hear,
are "numbers", it is the numbers we fear!

The number of people sick,
It is why on computers we click.
The numbers of people lost,
are like blankets of cold frost.

13. Censors, Wheels and Brooms

April 6th, 2020

The coronavirus quickly spread,
And a rise in cases, people dread.
Our housekeeper could not enter our home for her tasks,
especially with a dearth of masks.

Without the housekeeper in our home,
it is up to us to clean our home.
The new, complex robotic vacuum has shown a ray of hope,
so, we do not have to scrub the whole house with soap.

With such a confusing manual,
it was not a known ritual,
to vacuum or not it chose,
or else it will run over our toes!

The mishap of the day:
The robot chewed its way,
through all the wire.
My dad's head was on fire!

How foolish was I,
to leave out wires? Why?
The robot flipped with shock,
and I was on the chopping block.

The verdict sounded:
I was being grounded.
What a foolish robot,
in the wires it got caught.

Thank you housekeepers, your work is flawless!
You present to us, a home fresh and spotless.

Without you it is messy as a bird's nest.
Housekeepers, you are the best!

14. Health Vs. Beauty

April 7th, 2020

After weeks of an unkept look,
such tangled locks cannot be took.
People peer in the mirror and say, "Oh my gosh!"
"I look the opposite of posh!"

So, they open the barber shop,
more COVID cases will pop.
But such a comfort is a manicure,
only narcissism it will cure.

You may be sick in bed,
but, hey, you look great with your hair red!
You may never see your family again,
But tiny pig tails you have ten!

15. The Virus Brought My Friend Back

April 8th, 2020

I moved away after elementary school.
Away from friends, I cried a pool.
We promised to keep in touch,
but we never spoke much.

Lockdown has given us time.
To call friends, it is now prime.
So away from the daily track,
now we could call friends back.

The call I was waiting for all year,
finally came today, here!
I picked it up with no hesitation.
Inside my head there was a celebration.

I said, "Hello!" when I picked up.
Then she said, "what's up?"
So, we talked for half an hour.
The conversation was sweeter than a flower!

We talked about online schools.
We talked about COVID's rules.
We talked about board games.
We talked about friends' names.

I was so happy about her call.
It made me dance down the hall.
She agreed to call again the next day.
Now my sorrow was far away!

The phone conversation I had with my best friend from elementary school.

16. Crazy! Crazy! COVID

April 9th, 2020

This corona virus mess,
has given my family stress.
That causes many a mistake,
More than what we usually make.

Once, a gallon of milk was spilled.
When we're usually very skilled!
Once a yummy dish fell into the soup,
that made our heads droop.

Once clean clothes went into the washer,
and the dirty in the hamper.
I hope COVID goes away,
so, we can have a normal day!

17. Cooking during Pandemic

April 10th, 2020

When I'm stuck at home,
where will I roam?
To the kitchen, I went,
to mix, match and invent.

My mom is a great cook,
so, from out of the book,
she whips up many a dish,
according to my wish.

When I'm stuck at home,
and I compose a poem,
my dad agrees to buy sweets,
and my mom makes many treats.

My dad gave me an Oreo,
When he usually says, "No!"
My mon made a fat puri*.
"Fantastic," said I, the jury.

When I'm stuck at home,
I enjoy delicacies from Chile to Rome.

*Indian flat bread

My mom whips up many dishes and treats.

18. Egg Hunt with a Twist

April 12th, 2020

Today is Easter Sunday,
a fun day.
Even with the pandemic and rain,
I do not feel the dreary day's pain.

The egg hunt is not at the park,
the candy is hidden in the backyard, where no dogs bark.
All in my family's control,
Including where the eggs will roll.

I did not find every Easter treat.
The suspect I will meet.
The squirrel is the thief!
His stash must be as plentiful as the coral reef.

He found two of my treats,
now, by himself he eats.
Now his stomach must be upset!
This is why all the sweets I should get.

Squirrel thief enjoying my treat.

19. Culinary Experiments

April 12th, 2020

COVID has locked me inside,
to entertain myself I tired.
My mom cooked something nice,
with a side of rice.

My mom has been sautéing the unique,
From enchiladas to yogurt sauce that is Greek.
She fried fritters out of beans for soup,
so, they would no longer droop.

She cooked eggplant-spinach fry,
the excellent dish was a must-try.
So, while being locked inside,
we have many delicacies being baked and fried.

20. Lockdown Woes

April 13th, 2020

I've been at home for thirty days,
but I see no hopeful rays.
People are dying on beds and chairs,
for them let's say a prayer.

There is a very large workload,
on this devastating road.
The news gives ugly traps:
Garlic as prevention? Into fake news people tap.

The key is immunity,
so, of COVID you will be free.
Blackberries, honey and ginger,
will help you, I'm sure.

After all, when the vaccine is ready,
it will make your body steady,
to fight COVID, when it rises,
so, give your body super food prizes.

We are in this together!

21. The Sugar Cure

April 14th, 2020

Dine-in is a hazard,
so, there is nothing for our gizzard.
What to do to satisfy our craving?
Our home kitchen is opening!

A simple dessert is jalebi*,
it can make one go crazy.
Here is the recipe,
pair with hot tea.

This is how you prepare jalebi,
then of oil and sugar, you'll be free.
Take one cup of yogurt and one and half cup of flour,
add food coloring for orange power.

Whisk for good consistency!
It should be runny!
Pour batter into plastic pouch!
Cut the corner, so it says, "Ouch!"

Syrup is made with water, sugar and lime.
Sugar dissolves in no time.
First few drops are fast,
but the final drop is slowly last.

Then in hot oil,
squeeze the pouch, make a coil.
Fry, flip, fry, then for a minute it dips in syrup.
Hot jalebi coming right up!

*pretzel shaped South Asian dessert.

22. The Proud Produce

April 15th, 2020

While being shut inside,
I took great pride,
to grow new plants,
among the bees and ants.

I have grown a potato plant,
rich harvest it did not grant.
It was less than foot tall,
and the potatoes it bore were small!

I grew a mint plant too,
the leaves it sprouted were never few.
It grew tall and strong,
it will garnish my dishes a year long.

23. True Patriot

April 16th, 2020

A patriot is one who,
helps their country through,
a great problem.
Hurrah for them!

A popular image is of a soldier,
their country they fight for.
Now the medical and essential workers are patriots too.
They help human kind wherever COVID sprew.

Doctors cure the ill.
Essential workers bring necessities and pill.
Without their devotion,
the virus would cause more commotion.

SUPERHEROES
PRESCRIPTION

24. Go, Birdie, Go!

April 17th, 2020

Badminton, I have been playing,
While for the vaccine I am waiting.
My birdie will lose all its feathers, one after the other.
The racquet doesn't approve either.

My racquet has many a scratch,
from my every match.
The birdie is bent out of form,
like it has been through a storm.

Even though the equipment doesn't cooperate.
I'll give badminton a five-star rate.
To play with my family members, is enjoyable,
but with friends it's more desirable.

25. Extreme Measures

April 18th, 2020

COVID has kept me indoor,
so, I am wondering to the core.
What will people do,
so, COVID doesn't get them too?

Some to drink bleach, they try.
Sick or not they will die.
Some swallow UV light against the virus.
To me, they're as smart as a walrus.

They try the impossible,
yet they refuse the possible.
Why can't they socially distance?
Maybe they need assistance.

26. Digital Days

April 19th, 2020

Everyday I do school, online,
even though I don't find it fine.
I do it anyway,
every single day.

Some opt out of online school.
Busy parents can't help with each grammar rule.
It is good that, we have an education,
even through this tough situation.

We have many a video chat.
Teachers educate us on this and that.
Why not participate,
when there is *nothing* on your plate?

Hey, friends, please don't opt out.
Do not shout and pout.
Everything is done on a chrome book,
so, why do you have an angry look?

School is bundled up and handed to you,
although the way is new!

27. Humanity's Heroes

April 20th, 2020

It was an epidemic,
now it's a pandemic.
In China it started,
from there, it has departed.

Europe, USA!
Many lives it has taken away.
Over Asia it has spread.
It has also deprived many of bread.

Many are struggling to keep a roof over their head.
On the virus map, some countries are marked with red.
Even though, through hard times we go,
we have found many a hero!

Doctors work hard every day.
Necessities are delivered without delay.
so, even though many lives are lost,
and the numbers through the roof have crossed…

We still have hope,
through this situation, we will cope.
We will get through this,
And the heroes hard work, shan't be dismissed.

Corona virus attacks the Mother Earth.

28. Earth Day!

April 22nd, 2020.

Oh! Mother Earth.
You gave us so much from your hearth.
You gave us our lives,
and taught plants and animals to thrive.
You gave us the secret of fire,
still it doesn't quench human desire.
You gave a great blue sky.
You gave produce to try.
You gave us every tree.
You gave air to breathe free.
But we filled with smoke the clean air,
it is like, we don't care.
We chop down every wood.
We divided land and over others we stood.
So, we give you Earth Day,
for the land and sea, you lay.
We're sorry for what we've done.
We promise to recycle a ton.
We'll reduce our trash,
so, the ocean isn't a plastic mash.
We will give plants and animals what they deserve.
You are our home; you we will preserve!

Apologies Mother Earth.

29. Hooray for Teachers!

April 23rd, 2020.

I am doing online school,
but it has the same rule,
about work, behavior and such.
And, we are still learning about the Dutch.

Online school has done much.
The students are in its clutch.
It is still work, quizzes and tests,
along with all the rest.

On the computer, we've chats,
but some truants don't even do that.
I turn in everything,
Or my "late" bell will ring!

Although I should be grateful,
Because through these hard times we all pull.
Online school is a success because of the teachers.
Hooray! for tutors, educators and lecturers.

30. Pots of Paint

April 24th, 2020.

Before the shelter in place,
This activity put a smile on my face,
to head to the store "All Fired Up,"
and paint a ceramic cup.

Now the artwork sits still,
on my window sill.
Painted cups with many a pretty flower,
From when going out, was in my power.

I wish I could go back,
to see their stocked colorful rack.
I wish I could paint everyone.
It would be so much fun!

31. Walks in the Moonlight

April 25th, 2020.

To get some fresh air,
even though the owl at us will stare.
My family goes for a walk at night,
in the moonlight.

When no one is around,
when sleeps the hound,
we go to stretch our legs,
after a dinner of eggs.

There is no soul about.
Only us and the crickets are out.
So, COVID does not pose a risk;
so, to our house, we will not whisk!

32. Social Un-Distancing

April 26th, 2020.

In the cul-de-sac, around noon,
it sounded like pouring monsoon.
So, I stepped outside,
and it was nothing in my pride.

About a dozen kids were together,
In the nice, sunny weather.
Dumping buckets of water here and there,
they were riding their bikes everywhere!

There was no social distancing,
all playing in a ring.
Even adults, out of their houses, had stepped out.
Even toddlers were about!

Social distancing, there was none,
they were having fun.
Why am I unwillingly stuck at home,
if soaking wet they can roam?

33. History's Lessons

April 27th, 2020.

The novel corona virus pandemic,
in human history, is gigantic.
Along with the plague and the spanish flu,
another event to endure through.

Survivors will tell the tale,
as historians, stating how others did fail.
Alas! The others, a just a number,
and an example of the modern world's blunder.

Once this goes into the history book,
and many historians have taken a look,
this is a mistake to learn from,
and to make sure, again it does not come.

34. Clean Hands

April 27th, 2020.

A new soap is necessary,
also, hand sanitizers people carry.
Most do not ring a bell,
all persuade you, to, which cleans well.

Which one will you buy?
All seem good to try.
You try one that's cheap.
Your wallet cheers, your hands weep.

Cheap is bad, chemicals are harsh,
like washing in a mosquito marsh.
You hands cry, soapy and wet,
you will get skin disease, I bet.

So, get one that is soft and cleans well.
One that has a heroic tale to tell.
Your wallets smiles, your hands cheer,
your hands will not shed a tear.

A variety of soaps to choose from.

35. Wish List

April 29th, 2020.

Once the vaccine is out,
and people are out and about,
I wonder, what to do first?
Where will I satisfy my thirst?

First, I will go to school,
and to hug all my friends, it will be cool.
Next, I will go to the grocery,
to run in the isles, I will be free.

Then, I will go to an Italian restaurant.
I will order the entire menu, anything I want.
Lastly, I will go the water park,
And on a fun-filled day, I will embark!

36. Painting while Waiting

April 30th, 2020.

COVID has locked me inside,
so, towards the easel I stride.
I paint in many a style,
my masterpieces, to the roof they pile.

I painted with gold and silver.
It was a shooting star falling out of quiver.
I painted a meteor shower,
the picture gave the canvas artistic power.

I painted trees under the moon.
The moon light was as bright as noon.
This is what I've decided to do,
until COVID bids adieu.

Meteor shower on a moonlit night.

37. Staycation

May 3rd, 2020.

I want to go on a vacation,
amongst this confusion.
But cramped are planes, so is the train,
and driving for hours is a pain.

So, about warm beaches, I think,
and about the ice-skating rink.
How about a vacation at home?
while you play a bass or a trombone.

Many have got a pool,
and will play once finished with school.
Also, a hot jacuzzi,
instead of an ocean liner at sea!

This summer vacation,
will be milestone for the nation.
Everyone will be at home,
Instead of going to Hawaii or Rome.

38. War of the Stars

May 4th, 2020.

Everyone says, "May the 4th be with you!"
They dress up like the Star Wars crew.
A day dedicated to a movie?
How can this be?

There are much better movies that Star Wars.
Just waving swords really bores.
Lion King, Frozen, Harry Potter and Home Alone,
should be sitting on the throne.

What does Star Wars provide?
Just a large-eared-creature with green hide.
What kind of name is Skywalker?
Sorry, Star Wars fan, I am not a viewer.

Let all the champions have a tournament.
So, the viewers and fans do not lament.
Get ready, Simba, Elsa, Harry, Kevin and Luke.
Who will win? Will they win by merit or fluke?

39. Jewel of the Skies

May 5th, 2020.

COVID, unfortunately, has conquered the Earth,
from Los Angeles to Perth.
So, for reassurance I look to the sky.
Simply by the beauty of the sun and moon, I cry.

The universe is so pretty, it made me wonder,
if such celestial bodies had a maker.
The Jeweler cut and polished all the planets with care,
and that is why, this poem with you, I share.

There was once a jeweler,
who thought no end to himself.
He always boasted the best gems,
were on his shelf.

He would always argue,
which jewels were more fine.
He would always scream,
"No! The best ones are mine."

Then a fine astronomer,
said with glee,
"Why show your bits of carbon,
when there is a much better Jeweler, we all see."

I know someone has diamonds,
which are shinier than light.
So, why about your petty rocks,
do you fight?

When you go to meet this good gem,
make sure you wear spectacles.
The jewel itself is so bright,

his light itself is a spectacle.

So, when the solar eclipse occurred,
the sky became dark,
the birds called a drumroll,
as he presented a white ark.

The jeweler's eyes teared,
such a beauty he had never seen.
Not a speck of yellow,
it was so very serene.

The astronomer said,
"Do not puff your chest."
You are a mere spelunker,
when compared to the cosmos's best!

40. Tribute to the Heroes

May 6th, 2020.

To all who have a lost a loved one,
who hear just echoes of those days of fun,
who are shedding a bitter tear,
full of sadness, grief and fear.

My condolences to all those who,
fought COVID through and through.
But they died fighting and helping,
so, they deserve recognizing.

Like Dr. James A. Mahoney, gave up his life,
working through many crises and strife.
Even though, he was about to retire,
the compassion in his heart, never let him tire.

So, when the Earth is painfully silent,
and COVID rages, ever so violent,
let it be known that COVID has, sadly, taken away,
the best people of our day.

41. Go away, Metronome

May 16th, 2020.

I miss my violin class, when school is out,
my teacher assigns lessons, so we do not shout.
I pull out my metronome, to keep beat,
but I want to crush it with my feet.

I wish my metronome,
would go home,
right into its black case,
and never show its face.

I would play every note,
without its scolding beat or rote.
I would play free,
my metronome would let me be.

I had opened the case of my instrument,
because with boredom I was bent.
This homework is worse,
metronome, back in your purse!

Now that the pundit of beat is away,
the violin I will play.
I play my violin with glee,
since of the metronome I am free.

42. The Sweet Delivery

May 17th, 2020.

Eagerly, I waited for a delivery,
I was impatient but happy.
Then came a bright orange box.
It seemed to be full of rocks.

Out came pints of ice cream,
and the flavors were a dream!
There was dark chocolate, vanilla and almond brittle.
The ice cream was more than little.

Once in the freezer,
Knocked of the table was the salad ofcaesar.
Delicious was the banana split,
many more orders of ice cream were writ.

We are grateful to the delivery team.
These heroes supply everything from medicine to ice cream.
When the world has their lives stowed away,
they transported all the necessities without delay.

43. Hurricane Season

May 18th, 2020.

Hurricanes at sea, were found,
while still by the virus we are bound.
The disease will still harass us,
While the weather will also fuss.

Blowing wind, falling rain,
will damage and cause loss and pain.
Now we must hope and pray,
that sun shines a hopeful ray.

So, succumb we will not,
COVID and hurricanes will be fought.
We will come with victory,
COVID and hurricanes, be banished thee!

44. Critters In, Humans Out

May 19th, 2020.

In my backyard, I've been about,
I'm noticing plants, short and stout.
I can't help but see,
a large-toothed visitor is free!

In our backyard, there is a bunny,
who thinks it is funny,
to munch all the plants into nothing!
Around the backyard it is running!

He nibbled the sorrels, from their green pride,
to so bare, the plants wanted to hide!
Then that plant-stomping furry beast,
Walked right up to the door for a feast!

People it was not scared of!
It focused on its only love:
to eat or trample over every leaf,
and leave the garden in a state of grief.

His appetite is not lame.
He sneaks beneath the fence without shame!
I will stop this visitor!
It will visit no more!

The virus has stopped people from being out and about,
so, the rabbits and other critters are out.
The birds flock in the dozens in any weather,
But only Zoom calls bring my friends and me together.

45. Closing

May 20th, 2020.

Today, is school's last day,
when I usually hug my friends and say "Hooray!"
My arms full of old supplies, flowers and candy,
while keeping pen and paper, for signatures, handy.

Today, arms empty, I simply type,
"Thank you and H.A.G.S.," a tear I wipe.
I think of the long summer ahead,
staring at a screen, now I dread.

Usually, after gifts and smiles, my teacher says, "Meet me next year."
"Of course," I say without fear.
Now, I hope that I can do so,
Even with a mask on and from a distance, I hope so.

I would be so happy to see them.
It would be like finding a gem.
Their company was always taken for granted.
During the shelter in place, their company is all I ever wanted.

Last day of school.

About The Author

Apala Banerjee

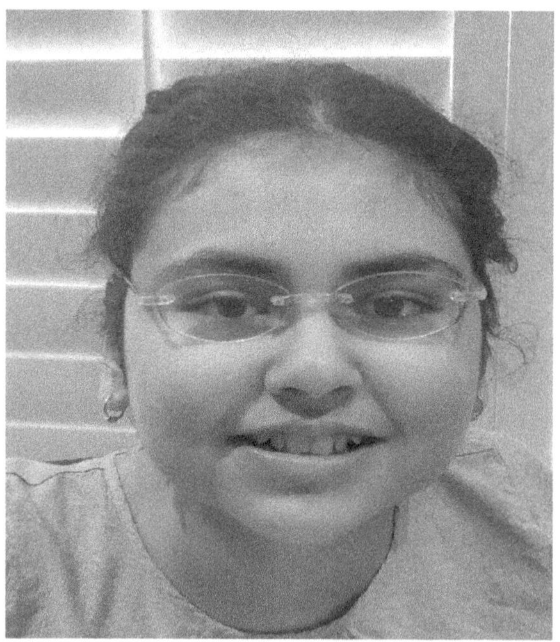

The poet is a rising 7th grader, who loves to read, play the violin and write essays and poems about the world around her. This is her first book of poems.